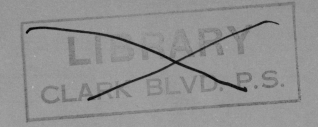

Those Green Things

Text by Kathy Stinson

Illustrations by
Mary McLoughlin

Annick Press
Toronto, Canada M2M 1H9

What are those green things?

What green things?

Those green things in the laundry basket.

Those green things in the laundry basket are your socks.

Oh, I thought they were lizards eating my T-shirts.

What are those green things?

What green things?

Those green things under my bed.

Those green things under your bed are last week's pyjamas.

Oh, I thought they were giant frogs Matthew squashed when he was jumping on my bed.

What are those green things?

What green things?

Those green things in my scrambled egg.

*Those green things in your
scrambled egg are spinach.
It's an omelette.*

Oh, I thought they were bugs and worms that weren't ripe yet.

What are those green things?

What green things?

Those green things in the closet.

Those green things in the closet are garbage bags full of old clothes.

Oh, I thought they were lumpy bumpy monsters hiding until I came to find my boots.

What are those green things?

What green things?

Those green things on the windowsill.

Those green things on the windowsill are your crayons. You left them there and they melted in the sun.

Oh, I thought they were the green beans Anna wouldn't eat at dinner yesterday.

What are those green things?

What green things?

Those green things in the garage.

Those green things in the garage are the garden hoses.

Oh, I thought they were slithery snakes sneaking through the window.

What are those green things?

What green things?

Those green things on the porch.

Those green things on the porch are Martians.
They are coming to take me to Mars so you
can't ask me any more questions about
those green things.

What green things?

Those green things
   in the laundry basket.

Those green things
   under your bed.

Those green things
   in your scrambled egg.

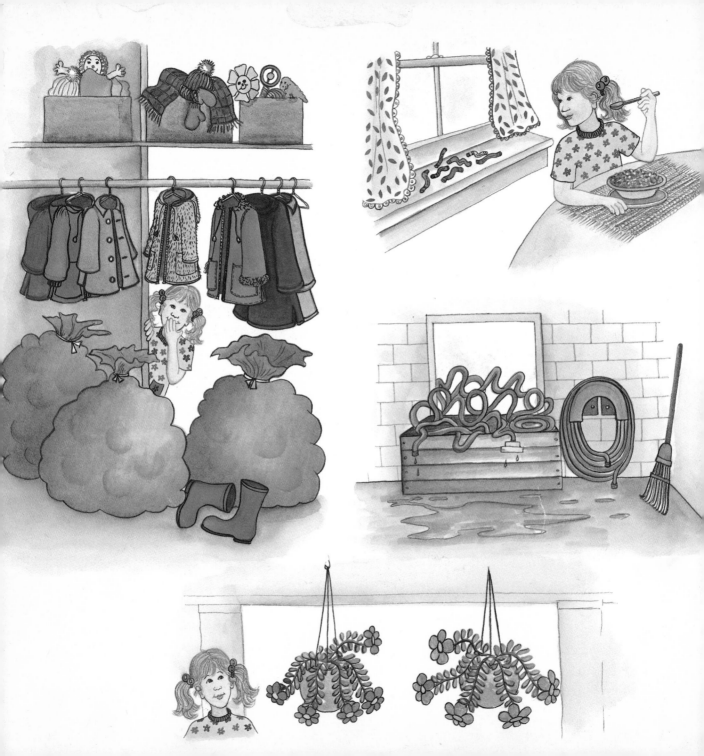

Those green things
in the closet.

Those green things
on the windowsill.

Those green things
in the garage.

Those green things
on the porch.

Mom?

Yes?

What are those green things
in your sandwich?

© **1985 Kathy Stinson (Text)**
© **1985 Mary McLoughlin (Art)**
All rights reserved
Third Printing, March 1987
Canadian Cataloguing in Publication Data

Stinson, Kathy.
    Those green things

ISBN 0-920303-40-4 (bound). – ISBN 0-920303-41-2 (pbk.)

1. Children's stories, Canadian (English). *
I. Title.

PS8587.T56T46 1985   jC813'.54   C85-099290-7
PZ7.S74Th 1985

Annick Press gratefully acknowledges the contribution
of the Canada Council and the Ontario Arts Council

Distributed in Canada and the USA by:
Firefly Books Ltd.,
3520 Pharmacy Avenue, Unit 1-C
Scarborough, Ontario
M1W 2T8

Printed and bound in Canada by D.W. Friesen & Sons, Altona, Manitoba